Welcome to
The Giggle Club

The Giggle Club is a collection of picture books made to put a giggle into early reading. There are funny stories about a contrary mouse, a dancing fox, a turtle with a trumpet, a pig with a ball, a hungry monster, a laughing lobster, an elephant who sneezes away the jungle and lots more! Each of these characters is a member of **The Giggle Club**, but anyone can join: just pick up a **Giggle Club** book, read it and get giggling!

Turn to the checklist on the inside back cover and tick off the Giggle Club books you have read.

TEE HEE!

HA HA !

JP

For Lee – A. R.

Mission Ziffoid

Michael Rosen
Illustrated by Arthur Robins

WALKER BOOKS
AND SUBSIDIARIES
LONDON · BOSTON · SYDNEY

"Guess what? My brother's got a spaceship
with four mega-blast booster rockets."

"Wow! That's good."

"No, that's bad. On the
way to Mars, the spaceship
exploded into a million bits."

"Gosh! That's bad."

"No, he escaped
in his ejector seat."

"That's good."

"No! That's bad. He crash-
landed on Ziffoid, a weird
planet zillions of miles away."

"Wow! That's bad."

"No, he landed on some lovely soft stuff and wasn't hurt at all."

"That's good."

"No! That's bad.
The lovely soft stuff
was a family of aliens."

"Ugh! That's bad."

"Oh no, that's good. The aliens thought he'd come to play football with them."

"That's good."

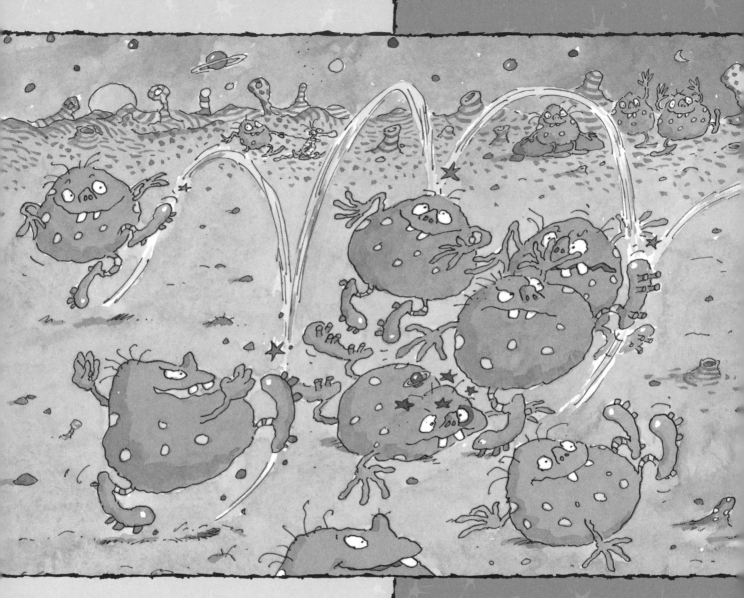

"No! That's bad.
My brother was the ball."

"Yikes! That *is* bad."

"No! That's good...

They kicked him into
their spaceship."

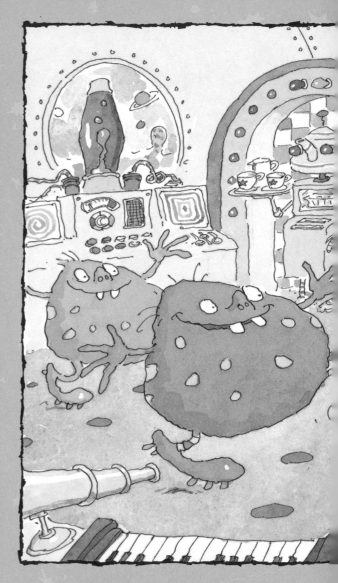

"Is that good?"

"No, that's bad. The aliens followed him inside."

"Oh, that's bad."

"No, that's good.
They said he could use
their spaceship to fly home."

"**That _is_ good.**"

"No, no, no! That is *bad.*"   **"Why?"**

The aliens came with him!"

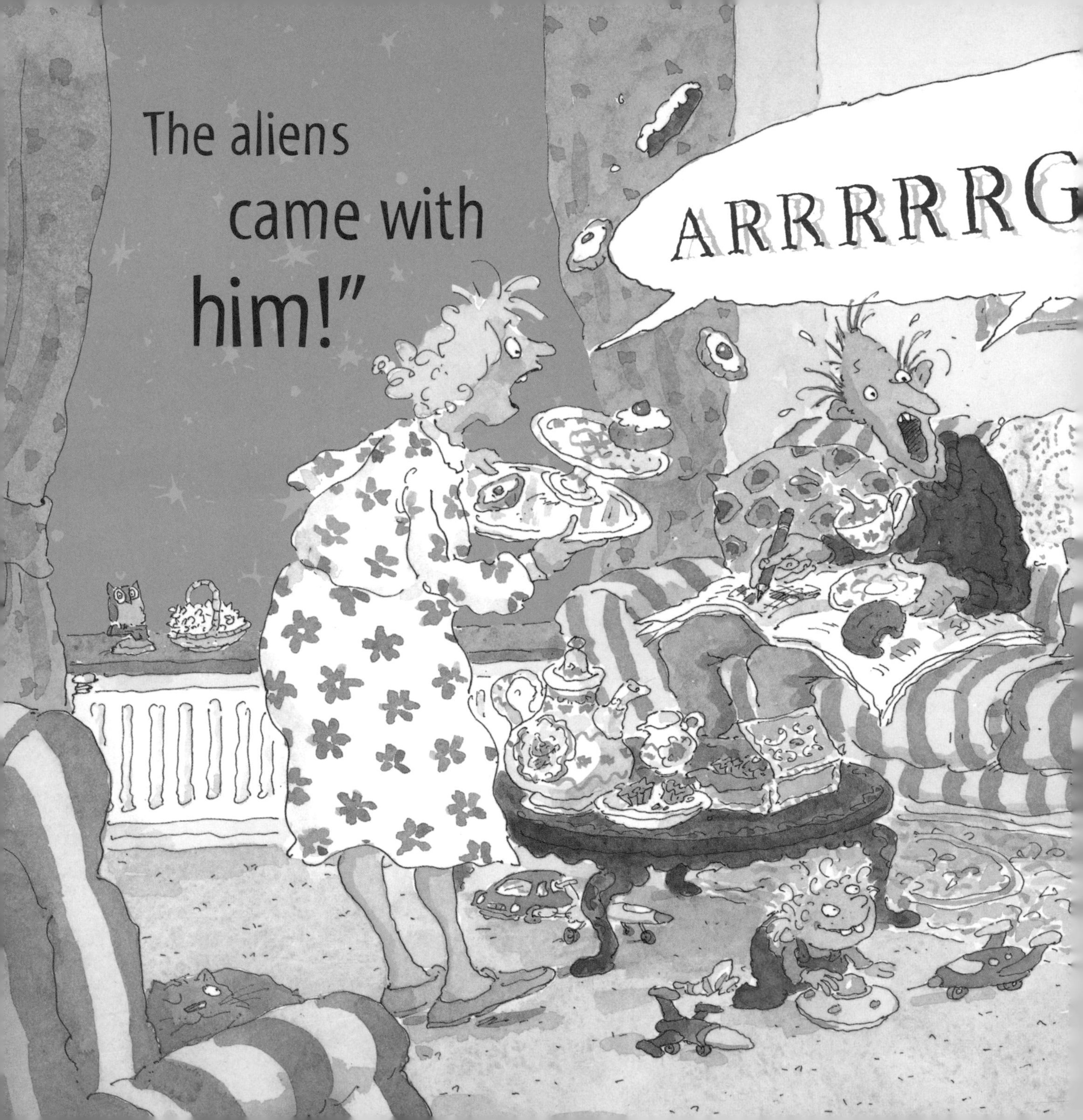

First published 1999 by Walker Books Ltd, 87 Vauxhall Walk, London SE11 5HJ

2 4 6 8 10 9 7 5 3 1

Text © 1999 Michael Rosen   Illustrations © 1999 Arthur Robins

This book has been typeset in Myriad Tilt.
Printed in Hong Kong

British Library Cataloguing in Publication Data
A catalogue record for this book is available from the British Library.

ISBN 0-7445-6942-7